The Care Bears Help Santa

by Peggy Kahn

illustrated by
Denise Fleming

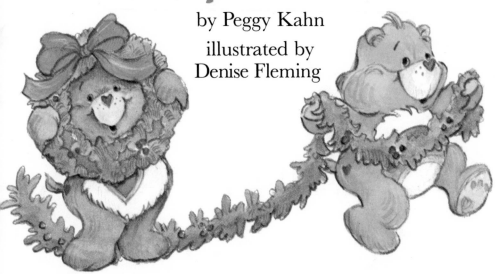

A Care Bear™ Book from Random House, New York

Copyright © 1984 by American Greetings Corporation. Care Bear and Care Bears are trademarks of American Greetings Corporation. All rights reserved under International and Pan-American Copyright Conventions. Published in the United States by Random House, Inc., New York, and simultaneously in Canada by Random House of Canada Limited, Toronto.

Library of Congress Cataloging in Publication Data: Kahn, Peggy. The Care Bears help Santa. SUMMARY: The Care Bears help Santa Claus when he gets lost in a fog on Christmas Eve. [1. Santa Claus—Fiction. 2. Christmas—Fiction. 3. Bears—Fiction] I. Fleming, Denise, ill. II. Title. PZ7.K12343Car 1984 [E] 84-3385 ISBN: 0-394-86807-2 (trade); 0-394-96807-7 (lib. bdg.)

Manufactured in the United States of America 1 2 3 4 5 6 7 8 9 0

It was Christmas Eve. The Care Bears were
busy getting ready for Christmas up in Care-a-Lot,
their magical land high above the clouds.

"I wish Santa would stop by Care-a-Lot so he could taste these cookies," said Wish Bear.

"It's not fair that Santa never comes here," said Grumpy Bear.

"You know Santa has to visit every child in the whole world tonight," said Tenderheart. "Maybe Care-a-Lot is too far out of his way."

"I guess you're right," said Grumpy.

Cheer Bear read *The Night Before Christmas* to the other Bears. Then they all settled down on their clouds to sleep.

Meanwhile, at the North Pole, it was so
foggy that Santa could hardly find his sled.
"I hope you don't get lost," said Mrs. Claus.

"Don't worry, my dear," said Santa. "The reindeer know the way. Come, Dasher! Come, Dancer!" And off they flew!

But the fog was so thick that the reindeer did get lost. In fact, they were right over Care-a-Lot! And before Santa knew it, his sled bumped into a thick cloud, and a bag of presents tumbled off.

The tinkle of sleigh bells woke the Care Bears.

"Look! Look! Santa's been here," said Funshine Bear. "And he's left a bag of toys for us!"

"Wait a minute," said Friend Bear. "These presents aren't for us. The tag says 'Smiley Children, Centerville.'"

"Oh, no!" said Good Luck Bear. "They won't be very smiley on Christmas morning."

"We'll just have to deliver the presents ourselves!" said Cheer Bear.

And so Cheer Bear, Friend Bear, and Good Luck Bear took the bag of presents and slid down, down, down—all the way to Centerville.

It was snowing. The Bears trudged down one street after another. It was getting later and later.

At last Good Luck Bear spotted the Smiley house!

The Care Bears found a very
worried Santa on the rooftop. He was
searching through the few bags left
on his sleigh.

"Is this what you're looking for?"
asked Friend Bear.

"The Smileys' presents! How can I ever thank you?"

"There's no need to thank us," said Cheer Bear. "But we would love to go down the chimney with you."

"You can go down the chimney FOR me!" said Santa. "I lost so much time looking for those missing presents, you'd be doing me a favor."

The happy Care Bears slid
down the chimney. They filled the
stockings that hung from the mantel.

"Let's stay until the children
open their presents," said Cheer
Bear.

The other Bears thought that
was a fine idea.

Because the Care Bears are very special bears, no one even noticed they were there.

"I got just what I wanted!" said Pat Smiley.

"Me, too!" said her brother, Robbie.

"We'd better get home now,"
whispered Friend Bear.

So while the children played with
their new toys, the Care Bears floated
out the window and up to Care-a-Lot.

Soon after the travelers returned, all the Care Bears heard sleigh bells and a jolly voice calling "Merry Christmas!"

It was Santa with a bagful of presents just for the Care Bears!

The Care Bears could hardly believe it—Santa himself!

"Before I go home," said Santa, "I thought I'd spend some time just eating cookies and having fun in Care-a-Lot."

Nothing could have made the Care Bears happier!

Santa and the Care Bears had a
wonderful time. When he climbed back
on his sled, Santa promised to come
back to Care-a-Lot every Christmas.
...And he has!